W9-APC-797

For Cecile Goyette—
an editor who likes odd ducks.
—J.D.

TRICKING THE TALLYMAN

BY JACQUELINE DAVIES

ILLUSTRATED BY S. D. SCHINDLER

ALFRED A. KNOPF
NEW YORK

THIS IS A BORZOI BOOK PUBLISHED BY ALFRED A. KNOPF

Text copyright © 2009 by Jacqueline Davies
Illustrations copyright © 2009 by S. D. Schindler

Visit us on the Web! www.randomhouse.com/kids

Educators and librarians, for a variety of teaching tools, visit us at
www.randomhouse.com/teachers

Library of Congress Cataloging-in-Publication Data
Davies, Jacqueline.
Tricking the Tallyman / by Jacqueline Davies ;
illustrated by S.D. Schindler. — 1st ed.
    p.   cm.
Summary: In 1790, the suspicious residents of a small town try
to trick the man who has been sent to count their population for the first
United States Census.
ISBN 978-0-375-83909-2 (trade) — ISBN 978-0-375-93909-9 (lib. bdg.)
[1. Demographic surveys—Fiction.
2. United States—History—Constitutional period, 1789–1809—Fiction.
3. Humorous stories.] I. Schindler, S. D., ill. II. Title.
PZ7.D29392Tri 2008
[Fic]—dc22
2007045488

MANUFACTURED IN MALAYSIA
April 2009
10 9 8 7 6 5 4 3 2 1
First Edition

HOW MANY PEOPLE LIVE IN YOUR HOUSE?
HOW MANY PEOPLE LIVE ON YOUR STREET?
COULD YOU COUNT THEM ALL?
WHAT IF YOU HAD TO COUNT EVERYONE
IN YOUR WHOLE CITY OR TOWN?
COULD YOU DO THAT? *HOW?*

There was a time when the United States was a brand-new country with a brand-new government. In order to make laws that were strong and fair, the government needed to know how many people were living in each part of the country. So in 1790 it sent out 650 marshals to tally (that means "count") the people—*all* the people. Without computers, cars, and calculators, these men set out on horseback to count *every single person* living in the United States.

How did they do it?

Well, see that fellow over there? The one who's drooping in his saddle? Take a closer look, dear reader. Because he is a tallyman, brave and determined to get his count! A rather tricky task, as you're about to discover.

When Phineas Bump rode into the town of Tunbridge,
he was heartsick, saddle-sore, and down on his luck.

Heartsick because he hadn't seen his beloved wife, Jenny, in three months. Saddle-sore because he'd been riding through the rooty woods. Down on his luck because his saddlebag was completely empty.

"How can I count the people without paper, ink, and quills?" he asked his horse, Blue. Blue, being a horse, didn't answer. She just stopped at the first house on the edge of town.

Phineas dismounted, mumbling, "I know, I know. Count them I must, and count them I will." He approached the door. *Knock! Knock!*

A woman opened the door—but just a crack.

"Madam," he proclaimed, "I am Phineas Bump, Assistant Marshal of the United States of America. By order of our Congress and Constitution, I am here to tally the people of this district."

"Begone, Tallyman," said the woman. "For we are a town that won't be counted." *Bang!* went the door in Phineas's face.

"Oh, ho," he said softly. "'Tis another one looking for a fight." Phineas liked a challenge. He stiffened his spine and raised his hand to the door. *Knock! Knock! Knock!*

The woman opened the door again—but only half a crack.

"Count you I must, and count you I will," said Phineas. "But for tonight I seek only a roof over my head. Might there be an inn nearby?"

"We have neither inn nor tavern. For we are a town that doesn't welcome strangers." *Bang!*

Phineas's smile widened. *Oh, ho! Hey-ya! A challenge, indeed.* "Perhaps I could sleep in the corner of your shed?" he shouted. But this time the door didn't open at all. Not one inch.

Phineas just laughed as he grabbed Blue's bridle and walked to a nearby stand of white pines. "Should we give up and go home, Old Blue?" he asked as he unsaddled his horse. Blue tossed her head. "That's what I think, too!" said Phineas. And he unrolled his blanket and lay down to sleep on the cold, hard ground.

Meanwhile, on the other side of the door, Mrs. Pepper called out, "Children, come quick! The Terrible Tallyman has come to Tunbridge."

"What's a Tallyman?" asked Mercy.

"Ooh, he's an awful scoundrel sent by the government," said Mrs. Pepper. "He counts every person in a town, and the more people he counts, the more money our town will have to pay."

"That's called *taxes*," said Boston.

Mrs. Pepper nodded. "Aye. And if there is another war, the government will know how many men we have and will steal them away to be soldiers."

"That's called *conscription*," said Boston.

"Aye, it is, my boy. Devils and deuces! Whatever shall we do?"

Patience burst into tears. Thomas hid in the wood box. But Boston said, "Don't worry, Ma. I've got a plan. *Oh, ho! Hey-ya!* We will be the town that tricks the Tallyman!"

In the morning, Phineas rose and brushed the pine needles out of his hair. "Count them I must, and—well, you know," he said to Blue before walking to the Pepper house.

Knock! Knock!

Mrs. Pepper opened the door grandly and offered Phineas the best seat by the fire. He pulled out an empty ink pot, a broken quill, and a letter. "'Tis from my wife," he explained. "But as I haven't any other paper, I will use this to make my record."

Mrs. Pepper stared sharply at the date on the letter. "Two months old. Has it been that long since you've seen her?"

"That long and longer," sighed Phineas.

Phineas scooped some ashes from the fire into the ink pot, mixed them with his spittle, and dipped the broken quill into the bottle. Then, in the margin of the letter, Phineas carefully wrote: "Tunbridge, October 18, 1790."

He turned to Mrs. Pepper. "Madam, your name?"

"Sarah Pepper."

"Your husband is—"

"Alas, gone," she said, clasping her hands and looking heavenward.

"My condolences, Widow Pepper. And how many children have you?"

"Not a one."

Phineas looked up. "I count three mattresses, a jack-bed with a trundle, and a cradle."

"Oh, but they are not for children," Mrs. Pepper explained. Phineas sighed. "I will mark but one," he said. "One free white female thus counted."

As Phineas marched outside and approached the door of the next house, Mrs. Pepper scurried close behind.

"That house is empty, Mr. Bump," she called out.

Phineas knocked on door after door, but every house was empty. Not a single person in the town of Tunbridge could be found. "Widow Pepper, are you telling me that in all of Tunbridge there is naught but one free white female?" he asked.

"'Twould *appear* so," said Mrs. Pepper, with a twinkle in her eye.

"Then I shall post the results, so that anyone who disputes the facts may come forth. And if none disputes them by tomorrow, they shall be declared fair and true, and so shall they stand."

Phineas nailed the results of his tally to the chestnut tree that stood in the town square.

"Blue," he said, "today I have been played for a fool. But tomorrow we shall see who has the last laugh."

At that very moment, Boston Pepper came running in. "Ma! Ma!" he shouted. "I've been to the next town over and it's not for taxes or soldiers he's counting the people! It's to figure out how many men we send to the new government."

"What do you mean?" said Mrs. Pepper.

"The more people he counts, the more men we'll send to the new government in Philadelphia. The more men we send, the more votes we get. And that's how we'll get the things we need, like good roads and regular mail delivery."

"Carp and cod!" exclaimed Mrs. Pepper. "We must trick the Tallyman into counting us again! But how?"

"Don't worry, Ma," said Boston. "I've got a plan!"

That night, Phineas again lay down to sleep among the tall white pines, still thinking of his Jenny and missing her more than ever.

The next morning, he rose. "Citizen of Tunbridge," he called out, "are the results, as posted, fair and true?"

"Not *entirely*," said Mrs. Pepper. "I think, sir, that you must count again."

Phineas shook his head. "Madam," he said, "that I cannot do. I am *entirely* out of paper."

Mrs. Pepper frowned. Paper was rare, indeed. The Tallyman turned to leave. "Wait! I will gather your paper," Mrs. Pepper declared. "By tomorrow you will have a ledgerful." Then she added in a whisper, "A *thin* ledgerful."

Phineas shook his head again. "But, Madam," he said, "I have neither quills nor ink."

Mrs. Pepper pursed her lips. "We will boil you six pots of ink and gather a dozen quills."

"But, Madam," said Phineas, "I could not possibly sleep another night at the White Pine Inn." He turned again to leave.

Mrs. Pepper squinted. "Constance Devotion runs an ordinary. You may stay there—free of charge."

"Oh, but, Madam," said Phineas, with a twinkle in his eye, "I'm afraid I'm not fit to be seen in such a fine place. My cloak, you see—"

Mrs. Pepper held out her hand. "Give it to me, Tallyman. I will mend it myself."

Phineas breakfasted that day on frumenty and mutton chops, dined on beefsteaks and baked beans, and supped on bread and butter and beer.

He slept in a feather bed, and in the morning, his cloak was better than new.

On the steps of the ordinary, Phineas found a wood-backed, leather-bound ledger with twenty sheets of paper sewn into it; six pots of the blackest ink; and a dozen turkey quills.

Well rested, well fed, and well supplied, Phineas knocked on Mrs. Pepper's door.

"Madam," he said, "I have come to count your family."

"Of course, of course, Mr. Bump! Do come in. Please meet my, *er*, recently returned husband, Mr. Samuel Pepper. And with him," said Mrs. Pepper with a wave of her arm, "my fifteen children."

"Seventeen souls under one roof?" said Phineas.

At the Swindle house, Phineas counted a husband, a wife, a brother, his wife, a father, and twenty-two children.

At the Gripe house, he counted a husband,

a wife, two cousins, and thirteen children.

And at the Thickpenny house, he counted a husband, a wife, two sisters, their husbands, four sets of grandparents, and thirty-seven children.

By sunset, Phineas had counted 1,726 people. He nailed the results to the chestnut tree. "Citizens—and animals—of Tunbridge," he announced, "I have posted the results of my tally. If none disputes them by tomorrow, they shall be declared fair and true, and so shall they stand." Then he walked through the evening gloom to his room at the ordinary, grumbling, "'Tis a tally not worth the paper it is written on."

Just then, Boston came bursting through the door of the Pepper house.
"Ma," he called, "I've been talking to a stranger who's passing through.
And he says the counting *is* for taxes and soldiers . . ."
    "Heaven help us!"
    ". . . *and* for sending men to represent us in the new government."
    "Both?" asked Mrs. Pepper.
    "Both!" answered Boston.

"Cheese and chowder!" said Mrs. Pepper. She pressed her hands to her temples. "If the Tallyman's count is high, we will owe too much in taxes and soldiers. If the Tallyman's count is low, we will have a weak voice in the new government. Who thought of this method?"

"The men who wrote the Constitution," said Boston.

"Clever devils, they be!" shouted Mrs. Pepper. "Oh, Boston. What is your plan now?"

Boston paced the floor and tapped his forehead. He pulled his hair. He rubbed his nose. He picked up the fire poker and waved it about. "Mother," he finally said, "I'm . . . working on it."

The next morning, Phineas slept late. The cows were milked and grazing on the common by the time he had packed up and saddled Old Blue.

As Phineas and Blue approached the chestnut tree, he called out, "Citizens of Tunbridge, are the results, as posted, fair and true?"

"Not *entirely*," said Mrs. Pepper. "I think, sir, that you must count again."

"Madam Pepper!" shouted Phineas. "I have been away from my dearest wife for three months. I will *not* stay in Tunbridge even one more day."

Boston pushed his way through the crowd. "Sir, if you will but count us one more time, I shall deliver to you a letter from your wife."

"Impossible," declared Phineas.

"I promise it," declared Boston.

Phineas stared at Boston. "Then I will count," he said. "ONE MORE TIME."

And so Phineas walked from house to house. By evening, he had counted 487 people. He nailed the results to the old chestnut tree and called out, "Citizens of Tunbridge, I ask you now, are the results, as posted, fair and true?"

Boston Pepper stepped forward. "Fair and true, they are, good sir." Then he pulled a letter from behind his back and handed it to Phineas. "The postal rider came through early this morning. He's been asking for a Mr. Phineas Bump through half the towns in the District."

Phineas broke the seal on the letter and read Jenny's words. Only Boston was near enough to see the tears of joy that sparkled in the Tallyman's eyes.

Phineas folded the letter and coughed once. "My dear Jenny is well," he said stiffly. "And she sends news. We are to have a child in the spring."

Boston turned to the shuttered houses and yelled, "His dear Jenny is well, and they will have a child come spring." A loud *"Huzzah!"* rose up from the town, and the people spilled out into the square.

"You know, Mr. Bump," said Boston, "I would have given you the letter even if you'd refused to count."

"And I, young man, would have counted you even without this letter." Then he raised his hand solemnly and said, "For count you I must, and count you I did. And now my job is well and verily done. *Entirely.*"

And so Phineas Bump rode out of the town of Tunbridge, no longer heartsick, saddle-sore, or down on his luck. Many more weeks of counting lay ahead of him, but now he traveled with a far lighter heart.

Mrs. Pepper and Boston watched as Phineas rode into the woods.

"Ah, Boston," said Mrs. Pepper, "I guess we are *not* the town that tricked the Tallyman after all."

"Sure we are, Ma," said Boston. "We're the town that tricked the Tallyman— twice! But then"—he winked at his mother—"we decided 'twas better to be fair and true. And so we were. *Entirely.*"

Author's Note

Counting all the people who lived in the United States in 1790 was a big job! The new nation covered nearly 1 million square miles. Almost everyone lived on farms, and there weren't many roads.

Secretary of State Thomas Jefferson took on the job of counting the people for the first census—with the help of about 650 assistants. They rode throughout the country, counting in every village and town.

When they began knocking on doors in August of 1790, they asked these six questions:
- What is the name of the head of the family?
- How many free white males sixteen years and older live here?
- How many free white males under the age of sixteen live here?
- How many free white females live here?
- How many slaves live here?
- Are there any other free persons living here?

In 1790 America, some people counted more than others, depending on how old they were, their race, and their gender. For example, each slave counted as three-fifths of a free person. Native Americans didn't count at all. Men over the age of sixteen counted as soldiers, but boys, girls, and women did not.

After nine months of counting, the tallymen were finished. *Whew!* They counted 3,929,326 people.

The census is still taken every ten years—just as the Constitution requires. But no tallymen ride on horses to count the people. Instead, the U.S. Census Bureau uses computers, telephones, and the mail to gather the information.

Today's censuses don't have anything to do with taxes or soldiers, but we still use the count to figure out how many Representatives each state sends to the government in Washington, D.C. It's also used to divide up the money the government gives to the states for things like new roads, bridges, and schools. If a state has a lot of people living in it, it gets more money. That seems fair, doesn't it?

In the year 2000, there were 281,421,906 people living in the United States of America. Think how long it would have taken poor Phineas to count them!

*Sharp-eyed readers will note that Tunbridge is an actual town in Vermont, which was the only state that didn't begin its count until 1791.